P9-DOE-800

The Strange Case of Dr. Jekyll and Mr. Hyde

Retold from the Robert Louis Stevenson original by Kathleen Olmstead

Illustrated by Jamel Akib

Sterling Publishing Co., Inc.
New York

Library of Congress Cataloging-in-Publication Data

Olmstead, Kathleen.
  The strange case of Dr. Jekyll and Mr. Hyde / retold from [the] Robert Louis
Stevenson original ; abridged by Kathleen Olmstead ; illustrated by
Jamel Akib; afterword by Arthur Pober.
    p. cm.—(Classic starts)
Summary: An abridged version of the tale of a kind and well-
respected doctor who can turn himself into a murderous madman by
taking a secret drug he has created.
ISBN 1-4027-2667-8
[1. Horror stories.] I. Title: Strange case of Doctor Jekyll and Mister Hyde.
II. Akib, Jamel, ill. III. Stevenson, Robert Louis, 1850–1894.
Strange case of Dr. Jekyll and Mr. Hyde. IV. Title. V. Series.

PZ7.O515Str 2006
[Fic]—dc22

                                                                2005015518

                          2 4 6 8 10 9 7 5 3

                   Published by Sterling Publishing Co., Inc.
                  387 Park Avenue South, New York, NY 10016
                      Copyright © 2006 by Kathleen Olmstead
                   Illustrations copyright © 2006 by Jamel Akib
                     Distributed in Canada by Sterling Publishing
                  $^{c}/_{o}$ Canadian Manda Group, 165 Dufferin Street
                       Toronto, Ontario, Canada M6K 3H6
           Distributed in the United Kingdom by GMC Distribution Services,
          Castle Place, 166 High Street, Lewes, East Sussex, England BN7 1XU
              Distributed in Australia by Capricorn Link (Australia) Pty. Ltd.
                     P.O. Box 704, Windsor, NSW 2756, Australia

            Classic Starts is a trademark of Sterling Publishing Co., Inc.

                              Printed in China
                             All rights reserved
                           Designed by Renato Stanisic

                  Sterling ISBN-13: 978-1-4027-2667-5
                       ISBN-10: 1-4027-2667-8

        For information about custom editions, special sales, premium and
            corporate purchases, please contact Sterling Special Sales
        Department at 800-805-5489 or specialsales@sterlingpub.com.

CONTENTS

v

CHAPTER I

The Door

⌒

It was often said that Mr. Utterson was very quiet for a lawyer. He was happier listening to others talk than talking himself. He did not brag or boast about his work. He did not spend too much time thinking about himself. Quite simply, he was a rare and admired man.

His clients were the misfits of society. They were people who often lived and worked on the wrong side of the law. Mr. Utterson always minded his own business and kept his distance, though. He merely did his job. He prepared wills and arranged finances—and turned a blind eye to everything else. He was careful never to get involved. Mr. Utterson was a man of order and routine. He never seemed to do anything even remotely exciting. In fact, he felt quite uneasy if anything was out of place. His schedule was set and he did not like the idea of change. He loved the theater, but he had not gone in over twenty years. He loved bridge, but he never played. The truth was that many people considered Mr. Utterson to be dreary, dusty, and cold.

Yet, Mr. Utterson was a well-loved man. His friends saw a different side to him. They saw a special spark in his eye. They knew him to be a kind, concerned, and caring man. He was favorite guest at dinner parties. He could always be counted on to listen to problems and offer wise advice. He was considered a dear, trusted friend by any who knew him.

Mr. Utterson's friends were relatives or men

that he had known for many, many years. He did not look outside his small circle for new friends. This suited his need for order and structure. So, each and every Sunday Mr. Utterson joined his cousin Mr. Enfield for a walk. They had been meeting for their Sunday walks for many years. So many years, in fact, that they had lost count.

They must have looked a strange pair to all who passed them. The two men spoke very little while walking side by side. They walked in silence, hands in pockets, each swinging walking sticks by their sides. When they happened to see a friend along the way, they seemed overjoyed for the distraction. They always urged the friend to join them on their journey. Looks can be deceiving, however. The men enjoyed their Sunday walks a great deal and refused to let anything delay them.

It was on one of their walks that Mr. Utterson and Mr. Enfield found themselves in a busy section of London. People filled the streets. Everyone, it seemed, was enjoying the sunny day. Mr. Utterson and his cousin turned down a quiet side street. Normally this street was full of people, but the shops were closed on Sunday. Therefore, the two men had the street almost to themselves. Unlike the rest of the neighborhood, which was run down, the residents and buildings along this street were doing well. The buildings were neat and clean with freshly-painted shutters and well-polished brass details. Mr. Utterson and Mr. Enfield admired the houses and shops as they walked past.

Two doors from the end of the block stood a building different from the rest. It had a battered doorway leading into a courtyard. The paint on the door was chipped, and the latch looked about to fall off. The building was two stories high. From what they could see from the street, it was in complete disrepair. The building looked neglected and abandoned. There were no windows on the wall facing the two men, only the door, without a bell or knocker.

They were standing across the street from the building. Mr. Enfield lifted his cane and pointed. "Have you ever noticed that door?" he asked his cousin. Mr. Utterson answered that he had. "It always makes me remember a very odd story," Mr. Enfield continued.

"Really?" said Mr. Utterson. "And what was that?" He looked at his cousin. Mr. Enfield was deep in thought.

CHAPTER 2

Enfield's Story

⟡

After some time, Mr. Enfield replied, "Well, it was this way. I was walking home very late one night. The path I took was completely empty. I saw no one for many blocks. The fog had set in, so there was no moonlight, only the streetlights to keep me company. I'll admit that I felt a bit scared. It's odd to be the only human in a dark and lonely area. At least, I thought I was the only person out that night. Quite suddenly, I saw two other figures on the street. One was a man walking away from me. He was rather short and stooped over. I was surprised by his speed. He moved very quickly and with a clear purpose. The other was a little girl about eight or nine years old. She was running along the cross street. Naturally the two ran into each other as the girl turned around the corner. The man knocked the girl down. It was horrible. He did not stop! He stepped on her leg and continued on his way. He barely seemed to notice her. The poor girl lay crying on the street and the man did not stop or even look her way! I realize that my description doesn't sound like much, but it was horrible to see. His actions were so cold. I yelled at the man and ran after him. I caught up with him quite easily and grabbed his arm. He did not resist as I brought him back to the screaming child. Actually, he looked perfectly calm. He wasn't the least bit bothered by his actions. Just then, the man gave me a look so ugly that I began to sweat. It was as though I had just finished exercising.

The girl's family rushed outside. She had been returning from going to get the doctor when this man knocked her over. Thankfully, the doctor wasn't far behind her in the street. He attended to the screaming child at once. He said she was more frightened than hurt. In any other circumstances, that might have been the end of it. But I had taken such a disliking to this strange fellow that I couldn't let it go. I wasn't alone in this feeling, either. The girl's family was similarly horrified, of course. But it was the doctor's reaction that struck me most. Whenever he looked at the man, the doctor grew sick and white with anger and hatred. At first, I thought he recognized this strange man, but I don't think that was the case. There was something about the man that caused so strong a reaction. Looking into this villain's face made you feel so uncomfortable that you wanted to turn away instantly. His eyes were lifeless and cold. His mouth was twisted into a cruel smile. I can only describe what I felt as horror. It was quite unusual."

"What did you do?" Mr. Utterson asked. "Did you call the police?" Mr. Utterson was gripped by this story. He needed to hear the ending. How was this strange man connected with the battered door across the street from them?

"We tried a different tactic," Mr. Enfield continued. "We told this man that we would spread the story of his cruel deed throughout London. Everyone would be talking about it. We warned him that if he had any friends or business, he would soon lose them. I expected this man to be sorry, but he seemed little affected by our comments. 'If you chose to make such a fuss about this accident,' he said to me coldly, 'then I have no choice but to obey your demands. After all, no gentleman wants to make a scene.' His voice was so calm that it gave me shivers. And then this awful man actually smiled! It was an awful, sinister smile. 'Name your price,' he said. With very little argument, the strange man agreed to pay the girl's family one hundred pounds. The doctor and I agreed to stay with the man and get the money. We followed him to the door—this very door that stands across from you and me right now—where he disappeared for a few minutes. He came back outside with a check for one hundred pounds. I examined it. I was shocked by the name on the check. It was the name of a well-known and upstanding citizen. Clearly this strange man had forged a signature or obtained it by unlawful means. 'Set your mind at rest,' the man sneered. 'I will stay with you until morning and cash the check myself. You will see it is good.' So, the doctor, the strange man, and I returned to my house, where we waited until the banks opened. It was a very uncomfortable wait. None of us spoke. The doctor and I watched this man with great curiosity. He stared into the fireplace the whole time. Finally morning arrived and we set off for the bank. I told the teller that I had every reason to believe that the check was fake. I was shocked to learn that it was real."

"Tut-tut," Mr. Utterson replied. He shook his head.

"I can see you feel the same as I do," Mr. Enfield said. "Yes, it is a sad story. The strange man that I met was a truly awful fellow, someone that you would never want to meet. He was frightening and evil." Mr. Enfield shook his head sadly. "And the man whose name was on the check was a man of merit and good standing in society. I cannot imagine what brought the two of them together. Since that night, I have referred to this building as the Blackmail House. I can only assume that the strange and wicked man holds some secret over the gentleman." Mr. Enfield drifted off into his own thoughts.

"And do you know," Mr. Utterson said, "if the

gentleman who wrote the check actually lives in this building?"

"I believe he lives somewhere in the Soho district," Mr. Enfield said absentmindedly. "I've watched this door from time to time," he continued. "It barely seems like a house at all. There are no windows on this side. No one comes in or goes out except, occasionally, that man. I've caught a few glimpses through the door and noticed that there are three windows facing the inner courtyard that are kept clean. And there is often smoke from the chimney, so someone must live there."

As the two men continued on their walk, Mr. Utterson was deep in thought. "Enfield," he said. "Would you mind telling me the name of the man who knocked the child down?"

"Well," said Enfield, "I can't see what harm it would do. It was a man by the name of Hyde. Edward Hyde."

Utterson took a quick deep breath. He recognized the name. "Ah, I see," he said. "Could you describe him to me?"

"As I said, he is not easy to describe," Enfield replied. "There was something unusual about him, something disturbing. I want to say horrible. I reacted with such strong dislike at the sight of him. Yet, I don't know why. His clothes were baggy and too big for him. He wore a tall hat and a cape. He had a slight hunch. No, on second thought, I don't think I can describe him. It's not that I forget what he looks like. I simply don't have the words."

"Are you certain that he used a key to get in the building?" Utterson asked.

"Of course," Enfield said.

"I know my questions must seem strange," said Utterson." The fact is, I don't need to ask the name of the other party because I already know it. You see, Enfield, the name Hyde is quite familiar to me. I cannot offer any details but I can tell you he is linked to a document I am preparing for a dear friend of mine, Dr. Henry Jekyll. If you told any lie or exaggeration during this story, please tell me. I must know all the facts."

"Every word I have said is true," said Enfield. He was slightly hurt that his cousin doubted him. He was not used to people, especially his cousin, questioning him. "Hyde had a key to the building. And what's more, he still has it. I saw him use it not a week ago."

Mr. Utterson sighed deeply but said not a word. He was thinking about that battered doorway and the courtyard beyond it. He already had concerns about this man Hyde. He now knew that he could not ignore this mystery any longer. Unfortunately, he had no idea what he should do next.

"Utterson," Enfield said. "I am sorry that I mentioned Hyde or this story. Let us promise never to discuss it again." He put his hand on his cousin's shoulder. It was clear that Utterson was very upset by the news. Enfield wanted to hear Utterson's story about Hyde, but he knew how much his cousin respected other people's privacy. Utterson would never reveal someone else's secret.

"With all my heart," the lawyer said. He was relieved that Enfield asked no more questions. "Let's shake hand on the matter and leave it be." The two cousins shook hands and continued on their walk. They spent the rest of their time together in silence.

CHAPTER 3

A Conversation with Dr. Lanyon

ॐ

It was Mr. Utterson's custom on Sunday nights to enjoy a good book by the fire and be in bed by midnight. On this night, however, Utterson sat down to dinner in bad spirits. He had too much on his mind and had a touch of indigestion. As soon as his plate was taken away, he went to his den. He opened his safe and removed some private papers. "The Last Will and Testament of Dr. Henry Jekyll" was written on the envelope. Mr. Utterson opened it and sat down. His brow was furrowed. Utterson was not pleased with the terms of the will. As a matter of fact, he had argued with Jekyll about its contents. The will stated that upon the death of Dr. Jekyll—or a disappearance of longer than three months—all of

the doctor's possessions and money should go to Mr. Edward Hyde. The lawyer thought it highly unusual for Jekyll to leave his entire fortune to one man. Utterson was one of Jekyll's closest friends, but he had known nothing about Mr. Hyde until Enfield mentioned him. Utterson was most disturbed by the phrase "or a disappearance of longer than three months." Why on earth would anyone include such a statement in his will? Did Dr. Jekyll think he might disappear? Utterson thought this was madness, but Jekyll had only laughed at him. There was nothing the lawyer could do but honor his friend's wishes. Now, however, Utterson was outraged to learn that this man Hyde was in fact a monster. Why would his good friend Jekyll be involved with such a man? With a heavy heart and a great deal of worry for his friend, he put the papers back in the safe.

Utterson could not think of going to sleep in such a state. He put on his coat and left for Cavendish Square, where his friend Dr. Lanyon lived. *If anyone knows about this man Hyde,* Utterson thought, *it will be Lanyon.* Lanyon, Jekyll, and Utterson had known each other since they were young. There was a time when they were insepa-rable. Many years had passed, though, and the old friends rarely saw one another. Lanyon and Jekyll, in particular, had gone their separate ways. Utterson knocked on Dr. Lanyon's door.

Dr. Lanyon greeted his old friend with a

hearty welcome. "It's been too long, Utterson," he said. "Where have you been keeping yourself?" Lanyon was a healthy, lively man with a reddish face and stark white hair. His house was well decorated with comfortable couches and chairs. Every room felt warm and welcoming. There was always a roaring fire and plenty of candlelight. Lanyon enjoyed company and long conversations with friends. He had a loud, booming laugh that was often heard echoing around his house.

They talked for a while about old times and what had happened since last they talked. Utterson said that his law practice was going well. Lanyon spoke of some of his patients and said that he was looking forward to retirement. Eventually, the lawyer brought up the reason for his late visit. "I suppose, Lanyon" he said, "that you and I must be Dr. Jekyll's two oldest friends."

"I wish we were younger friends," chuckled

Dr. Lanyon. "But I suppose we are. And what about it? I see little of him now."

"Really?" Utterson said. "I thought you had a lot of common interests. As doctors, the two of you always had so much to discuss."

"We had," came the reply. "But it is more than ten years since Henry Jekyll became too strange for me. He began to go wrong, terribly wrong, in my opinion. He had very odd and unscientific notions. Not only do I think that his ideas and experiments were unscientific, I believe they were unethical. He was moving toward very dangerous results. I simply could not continue to support him. Of course, as an old friend, I am still concerned for his well-being, but I want little do with him."

It was upsetting to hear that Lanyon and Jekyll had a fight. He wanted to ask about these dangerous experiments, but Utterson knew he should stick to the topic he really wanted to talk about. "Did you ever come across a man he knows named Mr. Hyde?" Utterson asked.

"Hyde?" repeated Lanyon. "No, I've never heard of him."

Utterson was disappointed. He had hoped Lanyon would provide a clue to the connection. The lawyer had seen little of Jekyll in the past few months. It was disturbing to know that Lanyon saw even less of him.

Utterson returned home shortly after this conversation and went to bed. It was not a restful sleep, though. The lawyer tossed and turned all night. He could not take his mind off Jekyll and this man Hyde. Was this criminal blackmailing his old friend? Enfield called it the Blackmail House and perhaps he was right. Was there something in Jekyll's past that he wanted to hide? Utterson thought this might be the truth. The doctor's youth had not been ideal. He had engaged in many wild activities. Utterson had warned his friend to be careful, but Jekyll had only laughed. The young doctor thought that no harm could come from a few adventures. Now, many years later, Jekyll was being blackmailed by this mysterious man. It pained the lawyer to think of his old friend awoken in the middle of the night by this monster, Hyde, demanding a check for one hundred pounds. And worse still, Jekyll had been persuaded to leave all his worldly goods to the blackmailer Hyde. Utterson worried for the safety of his old friend. He decided that he must meet Hyde face-to-face.

CHAPTER 4

The Search for Mr. Hyde

∽

For some time after, Utterson visited the doorway where Enfield had told his story. He stopped by in the morning before heading to work. He visited over lunch hours when the street was busy with shoppers. At night, when no one was around, the lawyer waited and watched. "If he is Mr. Hyde," Utterson thought, "then I shall be Mr. Seek."

At long last his patience was rewarded. It was a clear, dry night with a bright, full moon lighting up the street. There was no fog or rain. All of the shops were closed and the street was very quiet. Standing in a doorway, Utterson heard light, quick footsteps approaching. Before he even saw the dark figure turn the corner, Utterson knew it was Mr. Hyde.

Hyde was a small man. He wore casual clothes and a dark coat. His hat was pulled down low on his head. Utterson thought for a moment that Hyde was limping. But it was only his eyes playing tricks on him. Hyde had a strong, forceful walk. He walked straight to the door, pulling his key out as he crossed the street. He did not look like a burglar, or as if he was sneaking into the building. He looked comfortable. Hyde looked very much like a man going into his own home.

Mr. Utterson stepped out of the shadows and touched Hyde's shoulder as he passed. "Mr. Hyde, I presume?" Utterson said.

Hyde shrank back with a hissing gasp. He was

only startled for a moment, though. He appeared calm, but did not look the lawyer in the face as he answered. "That is my name. What do you want?" he said.

"I am an old friend of Dr. Jekyll's," the lawyer said. "My name is Utterson. I'm sure you have heard of me. It is a coincidence to run into you out here," Mr. Utterson lied. "I wondered if you would let me inside the house."

"How do you know me?" Mr. Hyde asked. He still refused to look Utterson in the face. He looked down the street or toward the door but not directly at the man standing in front of him.

"May I ask a favor of you?" Utterson said. He ignored Hyde's question. The lawyer thought it best to get straight to the point. Also, he felt the strong dislike and discomfort that Enfield mentioned. Something about Hyde brought about this reaction.

"Of course," Hyde answered. "What shall it be?"

"Allow me to see your face," the lawyer said.

Hyde appeared to hesitate. Then, after a moment or two of thought, he boldly looked the lawyer in his eyes. They stared at each other for several seconds.

"Now I shall know your face when we meet again," Utterson said. "It may be useful." Utterson spoke with a confident voice.

"Yes," returned Hyde. "It is good that we have met." Hyde spoke confidently as well. The two men stood face to face, almost daring the other to look away first. "It might be best if you had my address, too," Hyde added. He handed Utterson a card. It listed an address in Soho, a more dangerous part of the city.

My word, Utterson thought to himself. *Could he be giving me his address because of the will?* Utterson worried about his friend Jekyll. Did Hyde hope to collect his inheritance soon? He kept his feelings to himself, though. He thanked Hyde for his card.

"And now," Hyde said. "How do you know me?"

"By description," came the reply.

"Whose description?"

"We have common friends," Utterson said.

"Common friends?" Hyde asked. "Who are they?"

"Well, Dr. Jekyll for instance," said Utterson.

Hyde broke out into an awful, ugly laugh. His eyes were dark and cold. They did not sparkle or light up as he laughed. There was no joy. In the next moment, with amazing quickness, Hyde unlocked the door and disappeared into the house.

CHAPTER 5

Dr. Jekyll's Home

వా

The lawyer stood for a while by the door. He looked very uncomfortable. As he walked slowly away, he was lost in thought. *God bless me!* Utterson said to himself. *He seemed barely human.*

Utterson continued around the corner to the other side of the block. Most of the buildings on the street were divided up into apartments or offices. At one time this neighborhood had been home to large wealthy families. Many of these families had owned entire buildings. Only one house still had a single owner. That was the second house from the corner. It was also the last to show signs of wealth and comfort. The front door was newly painted. The knocker was polished and shiny. All the other buildings had dirty windows and broken gates, but this building was well taken care of and clean. Utterson climbed its front steps and knocked. A well-dressed butler answered the door.

"Is Dr. Jekyll at home, Poole?" asked the lawyer.

"I will see, Mr. Utterson," Poole said. The butler let Mr. Utterson inside and then went to look for his master.

Utterson waited in a large comfortable room warmed by a bright, open fire. This was one of the lawyer's favorite places in all of London. The room was decorated in dark, rich colors. The drapes were made of deep red velvet. The floors were covered in hand-woven

Persian rugs. The walls were lined with expensive artwork and well-stocked bookshelves. He and Jekyll had spent many evenings here in quiet, enjoyable conversation. Utterson's mood that night, however, was neither welcoming nor warm. He could not forget the face of the monster Mr. Hyde.

Poole returned with the news that Dr. Jekyll was not at home. "I'm afraid I don't know when he will return, Sir," Poole said. "He may be out for the rest of the night."

"I saw Mr. Hyde entering this building from around the corner, Poole. Through the door by the old laboratory." Utterson said. "Is that a good idea when Dr. Jekyll is away from home?"

"Mr. Hyde has a key," the servant replied.

"Your master seems to place a great deal of trust in Mr. Hyde," the lawyer said.

"Yes, sir, he does indeed," said Poole. "We all

have orders to obey him. Although, we see very little of Mr. Hyde on this side of the house. He mostly comes and goes by the laboratory."

Dr. Jekyll had bought the house many, many years before from another doctor. The previous owner had built a laboratory in the back of the house. The lab was a large room with high ceilings. Shelves and cabinets lined the walls. There were no windows in the room, only lamps and lanterns along the walls. There was an office above the lab where Dr. Jekyll could sit and work quietly. The office was much more welcoming than the lab. It had a fireplace, some comfortable chairs, and a window facing the main house. There was a courtyard separating the two buildings. Dr. Jekyll had not changed a thing in the lab. It was the main reason he bought the house. The cabinets and equipment were almost antiques, but Jekyll liked them. He often spoke about his desire to surround himself with beautiful things. It was important at home and at work.

"Well, thank you for your time, Poole," Utterson said. He wondered what Poole really thought of Mr. Hyde. The butler was always very polite. He would certainly never say anything bad about Dr. Jekyll. Utterson knew that Poole was very loyal to his master. As a matter of fact, all of Jekyll's servants were very loyal to him. He was considered a kind and fair man by all who met him. "Please tell Dr. Jekyll that I stopped by."

"Of course, sir," Poole said. The butler saw Mr. Utterson to the front door.

There was a cool wind. Utterson held on to his hat with one hand while he walked along the street. He was deep in thought. The lawyer was familiar with the less desirable members of society because many were his clients. He was aware of crime in the city and criminals who committed these acts, but he was very careful to never bring them into his life. His work was his work. He did not let it affect his personal life. He could never imagine bringing a criminal into his home. Utterson could not understand why Jekyll would let this dangerous man into his house. Perhaps his friend did not know about Hyde running down the little girl? Maybe Jekyll did not realize the danger he was in? Sadly, Utterson knew that this was not true. He knew in his heart that Jekyll was well aware of Hyde's unlawful activities.

By this time, the lawyer was very worried about his old friend and his connection to Mr. Hyde. It must be the ghost of some old sin that holds Jekyll prisoner. Why else would he deal with the likes of Mr. Hyde? Jekyll's family was very wealthy. He had always lived a life of luxury, despite his studies and experiments. He only worked because he enjoyed science. Utterson wondered about his own youth, if there was anything he might want hidden. He could think of nothing that would bring him such shame or fault. Utterson also worried that if Hyde knew of Jekyll's will—that he was to inherit all of the doctor's great wealth—he might do something to speed up the process. *If only Jekyll would let me help.* Utterson shook his head. This mystery was far from being solved.

CHAPTER 6

Dr. Jekyll Was Quite at Ease

∞

Two weeks later Dr. Jekyll gave a dinner party for a small group of old and dear friends. Mr. Utterson was among the guests, of course. Utterson was a well-loved guest at any dinner party. He was especially welcome at the end of the evening. Hosts enjoyed his dry wit and careful manner. The lawyer provided a calm break after a talkative dinner party. On that night in particular, Utterson made certain to stay after the others. He waited by the fire until everyone had left.

Dr. Jekyll took a seat across Utterson. He was a large, fit, smooth-faced man of fifty. He used to lead conversations and discussions in a lively manner. Lately, however, he preferred to listen quietly. Over the past year or so, Jekyll had grown more distant. He was colder and more removed. Some thought he appeared judgmental. They criticized him whenever he was not at a social function or dinner party. As a result, Jekyll became less and less social. His friends often remarked how rarely they saw him. There was a time when they had seen each other once a week, but now several months often passed without seeing the doctor. On this night, however, he seemed like his old self. He had a relaxed smile across his face while talking to Utterson. They sat drinking their tea before the fireplace.

"I have been wanting to speak to you, Jekyll," Utterson began. "You know that will of yours?"

"My poor Utterson," Jekyll said. "I never saw

anyone as distressed as you when you saw that will, except our good friend Lanyon when he spoke out against my unscientific theories. Or should I say what he called my unscientific theories. He's an excellent fellow, but I've never been more disappointed in a man."

"You know I never approved of the will," Utterson continued. He chose to ignore Jekyll's change of topic.

"My will? Yes, certainly, I realize that." The doctor spoke a bit sharply. The lawyer was surprised by Jekyll's angry response. "You told me so."

"Well, I'll tell you so again," said the lawyer. He was determined to have this talk with Jekyll. It was far too important. "I've been learning something of that Mr. Hyde."

The large handsome face of Dr. Jekyll grew pale. "I do not care to hear more," he said. "This is a matter I thought we had agreed to drop."

"What I heard was awful," Utterson said. He felt uncomfortable prying into Jekyll's business. This was not something he would normally do. Utterson was a popular lawyer among certain members of society because he did not ask too many questions. He did his job without digging too deeply into his clients' lives and actions. Jekyll was more than a client, though. He was Utterson's oldest and dearest friend. The lawyer knew that he must pursue the topic of Hyde or he would never forgive himself.

"I will not change my mind. You do not understand my position," returned the doctor. "My situation is very strange. Very strange, indeed."

"Jekyll," Utterson said. "You know me. I am a man to be trusted. Make a clean break of this business and tell me everything."

"My dear Utterson," Jekyll said, "this is very

good of you and I cannot thank you enough for your generosity. I trust you more than any man alive—even before myself—but I have no choice in the matter. I'll put your mind at ease, though. I can be rid of Hyde whenever I choose." Jekyll sat straight up in his chair. He looked his friend in the eye. The force of his stare seemed familiar to the lawyer. Utterson wondered where he had seen it before.

"If you can be rid of Hyde at any moment," Utterson said, leaning forward in his chair, "then I beg that you do so now." He tried to keep his voice calm but it was hard to hide his concern. "Please Jekyll. You must end your relationship with Hyde."

"I thank you for your concern, but remember that this is a private matter. Please, let it go," Jekyll said.

Utterson turned his gaze to the fire. He

thought for a moment. "I have no doubt you are perfectly right," he said at last. Utterson decided there was nothing he could do. He would have to trust his friend in this matter. He stood up to walk away.

"There is one point that I hope you understand," Jekyll added. "I have a great interest in Hyde, a very great interest. He told me that you met near the laboratory door the other week. I fear that he was rude to you. I am very sorry for that. He is a difficult man, I know. But I need your word that you will honor the terms of the will. If I should die—or disappear—please see that Hyde receives what is rightly his. It would be a weight off my mind if you promised."

"I can't pretend that I shall ever like him," Utterson said. The lawyer wondered if he would ever get his friend back. He wondered if Jekyll was now lost to this man Hyde.

"I don't ask that," Jekyll pleaded. "I only ask for justice. I only ask you to help him for my sake, when I am no longer here."

Utterson heaved a big sigh. "I promise."

CHAPTER 7

The Carew Murder Case

⌒

It was nearly a year later that all of London was shocked by a hateful and horrible crime. Mr. Danvers Carew, a well-known politician, was murdered. The details were few and startling. A maid in Dr. Jekyll's house had gone to bed at about eleven o'clock. Her room overlooked an alley that was brilliantly lit by the full moon. She sat at the window for some time, looking over the beautiful scene. Later, she told the police that it was the most peaceful night she had ever experienced—until she saw two men in the alley.

The maid noticed an old man walking through the alley first. He was well dressed and had a beautiful mane of white hair. She could see his face clearly in the bright moonlight. She thought he looked handsome and kind. Then she saw another man walking toward him. This second man was small and wore a heavy coat and dark hat. As they approached one another, the older man bowed to the second man. The maid thought that the older man was asking for directions. The old man held up a piece of paper and pointed down the alley. As she could see his face clearly, she knew he was calm and rather jolly. He even laughed. Then she noticed the face of Mr. Hyde. She recognized him as the sometime visitor of her master. Hyde held a heavy cane in his hand. He was swinging it by his side. All of a sudden, Hyde raised the cane above his head. The older gentleman took a step back, but it did not help. The maid watched in horror as Hyde swung the cane. The older gentleman fell to the ground.

The maid fainted. When she woke up several hours later, she ran to the police to report the murder. They responded at once. At first, they did not know the victim's name, but they discovered a letter on his body. It was addressed to Mr. Utterson. The lawyer was awoken from his bed in the middle of the night to identify the body.

He went with the police to the hospital where the body was waiting. His first thought was that Dr. Jekyll had been killed. He was very nervous and frightened for his friend. It took a great deal of courage for the lawyer to look at the body. He did not know what he would do if it was Jekyll. "I recognize him," Utterson said. "I am sorry to say that this is Sir Danvers Carew."

"No! This case will be in all the morning papers," the police officer said. He shook his head in amazement. "Sir, we are also hoping you will have some knowledge of the criminal." The police then told him the maid's story of Mr. Hyde beating Carew with his cane.

Mr. Utterson was taken aback. "Hyde, did you say?" He was shocked that Hyde would have a connection with someone else he knew, especially Sir Danvers Carew. He had been prepared for Hyde to have hurt – even killed – Dr. Jekyll, but not Carew. Utterson wondered if anyone was safe from Mr. Hyde. The lawyer looked quite ill.

"Yes, sir," the police officer said. "He used this cane as a murder weapon." The officer passed the walking stick to Utterson. The lawyer gasped. He recognized it as a gift he had given to Dr. Jekyll several years before. Jekyll must have given it to Hyde. Or Hyde had stolen it. Utterson did not mention this fact to the police. He knew that he was hiding evidence, but he was concerned for his friend. He wanted to talk to Jekyll first.

There was a more important matter at the moment, though. Hyde must be found and arrested. Utterson knew where to look. The lawyer still had the strange man's card in his wallet.

"If you will come with me," Utterson said, shaking his head sadly, "I can take you to Mr. Hyde's apartment."

CHAPTER 8

Mr. Hyde's Apartment

༄

Utterson took the police to Hyde's apartment in Soho. By this time, it was nine o'clock in the morning. The streets were full of people. Hyde's street was filled with closed stores and rundown buildings. Children wearing little more than rags sat on steps. Men begged for change on the street corner. Utterson wondered again how Dr. Jekyll had met someone from this neighborhood. He was also reminded of how much Hyde must want to inherit Jekyll's fortune. It would certainly allow him to move away from Soho.

A policeman knocked. A woman with silver hair answered the door. Her face was wrinkled and hard. The policeman asked if this was the home of Mr. Edward Hyde. She said that this was his home, but he was not in.

"He doesn't always stay here, you know," she said. "As a matter of fact, last night was the first time I had seen him in months." She was confused by the policemen's arrival. What did they want with Mr. Hyde? She could tell that something exciting had happened. Perhaps Hyde had committed some crime. She couldn't wait to hear all the details. She was already planning what she would say to her neighbors. "He was only here for about an hour, though," she added.

"May we see his rooms?" Utterson asked.

The woman looked at the lawyer—and the policemen behind him—and let them into the building. "I always suspected that man would find trouble," she said. "What has he done?"

Utterson and the policemen exchanged looks, but said nothing. They followed the woman up to Hyde's apartment. The rich warmth of Hyde's rooms surprised Utterson. They were decorated with great luxury and taste. Fine art covered the walls and mantelpiece. He recognized several of the artists and knew the paintings were quite costly. The lawyer suspected that Dr. Jekyll had helped decorate. He knew a great deal about art. The rugs were hand-woven. The curtains were made of dark, heavy cloth. Utterson also noticed the expensive china and crystal about the rooms. He never would have thought Hyde was the type of person to use such fine dishes.

The rooms were a mess. Clothes were scattered about the floor. Drawers were left open and overturned. Ashes from recently burned papers filled the fireplace. The police examined the remains and discovered part of a checkbook. Thankfully, they could still read the account information. The name "Mr. Edward Hyde" was clearly labeled.

"This will lead us to him," a police officer said. "All his banking information is here. We can wait for him at the bank and nab him when he tries to withdraw his money."

"It seems so careless that he would leave that information behind," Utterson wondered aloud. Although he had only met Mr. Hyde once, Utterson did not think he was the type to be so forgetful. He had seemed so sneaky when they met. *He must have been in a terrible hurry,* Utterson thought.

The police officer shrugged his shoulders. "The point is that we have him. Mr. Hyde will not slip away," he said. The police were convinced that the case would be closed almost immediately. They predicted that Hyde would be safely in jail by the next day.

"I do hope you're right," Utterson remarked. "Nothing would make me happier than to see the end of Mr. Edward Hyde."

CHAPTER 9

The Incident of the Letter

⌒

Later that afternoon, Mr. Utterson went to find Dr. Jekyll. Poole let him in and led the lawyer to the laboratory across the courtyard. "Dr. Jekyll is not feeling very well today," Poole said. "He prefers the quiet of the lab."

"Are you sure he's up for visitors?" Utterson asked. Jekyll was so rarely available these days. The lawyer was surprised that he would see him when sick.

"The doctor said that if you stopped by, I

should let you in straight away," Poole said. "Everyone else should be turned away."

Dr. Jekyll did not rise to meet his visitor. He remained by the fire, looking deathly sick.

"You have heard the news," Utterson said as soon as Poole had left them.

The doctor shuddered. "I heard it first thing this morning. They are talking about it all over London." Jekyll closed his eyes for a moment. "The police were here this morning asking what I knew about Hyde."

"I am asking you this question as your lawyer and your friend," Utterson said. "You have not been mad enough to hide this man, have you?"

"Utterson, I swear to God," he cried. "I swear to God that I will never set eyes on Hyde again. It is all at an end. And to be honest, he doesn't want my help. You do not know him as I do, Utterson. Mark my words. He will never be heard from again."

"You seem quite sure," the lawyer said. "I hope you are right. I should warn you that if there is a trial, your name may be mentioned."

Dr. Jekyll lowered his head. There were tears in his eyes. "I am quite sure that he is gone. I have received a letter. I don't know if I should take it to the police. I'd rather leave it with you and let you decide what to do. I trust you completely."

"Are you worried that the letter may reveal Hyde's whereabouts?" Utterson asked. He did not know why Jekyll was thinking about hiding the evidence. Was he still protecting Hyde?

"No. I have no concern about Hyde's fate, now," Jekyll said. "I am quite through with him."

His friend's behavior disturbed Utterson. He seemed quite upset. Jekyll was taking Sir Danvers' murder very badly. He must feel guilty for bringing Hyde into the neighborhood. "Perhaps you should let me see the letter," Utterson said.

It was written in odd, upright letters. It was stiff and awkward handwriting. It stated simply and clearly that Dr. Jekyll, his kind benefactor, should not worry, as he had means of escape. He was gone from the city and would not return. This message pleased Utterson very much. It was a great relief to know that Hyde was gone. "May I see the envelope?" Utterson said.

"I burned it," Jekyll said. "I wasn't thinking clearly. It doesn't matter, though. There was no postmark. The police wouldn't be able to trace it. The note was hand-delivered this morning."

"Shall I keep this letter and think about what to do?" Utterson asked.

"I leave it entirely in your hands. I have lost faith in my own judgment." Dr. Jekyll held his head in his hands.

"Tell me something, Jekyll," Utterson said. "The odd terms in your will, making Hyde your

heir in case of death or disappearance, were all his idea, weren't they?"

Jekyll nodded his head slowly.

"I knew it!" Utterson exclaimed. "He meant to murder you."

Once again, Jekyll shook his head. "It was nothing like that, Utterson. I could never explain it to you. It was something between Hyde and me that no one else could share. And no one else will ever learn. But I have learned a lesson! Oh, what a lesson I have learned." He put his head back in his hands and wept.

"One more thing, Jekyll." Utterson spoke in a soft voice. He did not want to upset his friend more. "Do you have any idea why Hyde did it? Was it a robbery or did he have other reasons?"

Jekyll did not lift his head from his hands. "No," he said. His voice was muffled. "I have no idea."

On his way out, the lawyer stopped to speak

to Poole. "There was a letter delivered today," Utterson said. "What did the messenger look like? I would like to find the person who sent it."

"I'm sorry, sir," Poole said. "We've had no mail today."

This news surprised Utterson. The letter must have come by the laboratory door, the one Hyde used to use. It seemed strange that Jekyll would answer a door himself considering his state of mind. The doctor said that he received the letter after the visit from the police. Perhaps the note had been written in the study. If so, that meant that Hyde was with Jekyll when he wrote it. But that would mean that Jekyll had lied to him. If he was willing to trust the lawyer with the note, why wouldn't he trust the lawyer with the truth? Utterson left Jekyll's home confused and concerned.

CHAPTER 10

Utterson Examines the Letter

Utterson made his way to his office. All the talk in the streets—in the entire city, for that matter—was about the murder of Sir Danvers Carew. Suddenly everyone knew the name Edward Hyde. It was hard for Utterson to mourn one person while worrying about another. His mind was swimming with questions and concerns. A fog had rolled into the city. One could not see from one corner to the next. London looked like a thick, gray soup. Utterson thought this weather suited his mood. Nothing was clear anymore. He understood nothing.

Mr. Guest, Utterson's assistant, offered his sympathies as soon as the lawyer walked through the door.

"It is awful news about Sir Danvers," Guest said.

"Yes, indeed," Utterson replied. "This man Hyde is mad, of course."

Utterson and Guest shared many secrets with one another. Their work demanded a great deal of honesty between them. The topic of Hyde and his connection to Jekyll had already been discussed. Guest had worked with Utterson in finalizing the strange will. The lawyer hoped that Guest would have a fresh point of view on the letter. He told his assistant about his visit to Jekyll and the note that Hyde had sent.

"I have a document here written in the killer's own hand," the lawyer said.

"May I look at it, sir?" Guest asked.

"I was hoping you could offer your expert advice," Utterson said. Guest studied the art of handwriting. He firmly believed that handwriting told a great deal about a person. "What can you tell me about this Mr. Hyde?" Utterson gave Guest the note.

Guest took his time looking over the note. At long last, he lifted his head from the desk. "Well,

sir," Guest said. "I don't believe he's mad. But it certainly is an odd style of writing."

The mailman interrupted their conversation. He placed the morning mail on Guest's desk and left. Utterson started to sort through the letters.

"Sir," Guest said. "Is that a letter from Dr. Jekyll?" Utterson said that it was. "I thought so," Guest exclaimed. "I recognized the handwriting. Is it something personal?"

Utterson quickly opened it. "Why, no," he said. He was confused by his assistant's eager questions. "It's an invitation to dinner."

"Would you mind if I looked at it, as well?" Guest asked.

The assistant laid the two pieces of paper side by side on the desk. He examined them both for some time.

"Why do you compare them, Guest?" the

lawyer asked. He was both curious and upset by his assistant's actions.

"Well, sir," said the clerk, "there are many similarities between the two. At many points both styles are identical. They have a different slope. That's all."

"That's strange," Utterson said.

"Very strange, sir." The two men looked at each other. They were not certain what all of this meant but they knew it was serious.

"I wouldn't speak of this note, you know," said Utterson.

"No, sir," Guest replied. "I understand."

That night Utterson locked the note in his safe at home. He thought it best if no one else had the chance to see the writing. *I never thought it possible,* Utterson thought. *Henry Jekyll forging a note for a murderer!* And his blood ran cold in his veins.

CHAPTER 11

The Remarkable Incident
with Dr. Lanyon

⌒

The police offered thousands of pounds for the arrest of Sir Danvers Carew's murderer. Mr. Hyde, however, was nowhere to be found. It was as if he had dropped off the face of the earth. Not one person had caught even a glimpse of him since the night of the terrible murder. Hyde was certainly the talk of the city, though. Vile stories of his cruelty and evil deeds were told on every street corner, office, and home. Each was more awful than the last.

Utterson thought this was a particularly

brutal case. But, oddly, the death of one man, Sir Danvers, resulted in the renewal of another man's spirits. Dr. Jekyll came out of hiding. He saw old friends again. He began hosting parties and attending social engagements. Utterson also noticed that Jekyll had even become more religious. The doctor had always been a charitable man, but was suddenly more devoted to his prayers and attended church services. For two months, Jekyll seemed healthy and happy. Many people commented on how relaxed and at peace he looked.

The dinner party that had been announced in the curious invitation was held on the 8th of January. Mr. Utterson and Dr. Lanyon were both guests. The two men noticed their host's happy face throughout the evening. He was clearly pleased to spend the evening with two of his oldest friends. Certainly he was remembering when the three had been the best of friends. Utterson felt a familiar happiness. He was confident that life was back on track.

On the 12th of January, though—and again on the 14th—the door to Jekyll's home was closed to visitors. On both nights Utterson dropped by unannounced. Poole told him that the doctor wished to see no one. When he was rejected again on the 15th, Utterson began to worry. Jekyll was falling back into his old pattern of hiding. Utterson was reminded of the days when Hyde had control over his friend. It was much worse this time, though. It was unusual for Jekyll to cut himself off so completely. Utterson decided to visit Dr. Lanyon. Perhaps the good doctor would have some advice.

Utterson was admitted into Dr. Lanyon's study. He was shocked at what he found. Something awful had affected Lanyon's appearance. He was pale and sickly and looked at death's door. Lanyon looked like he had aged thirty years in the week since Utterson had last seen him.

"My word, Lanyon," Utterson said as he stepped closer to his friend. He knelt beside the doctor's chair and took his hand. Utterson came here on a mission to save one friend. It shocked him to think he might have to worry about saving two. "Whatever could be wrong? Where did this sickness come from?"

Lanyon shook his head. "No," he said. "I am not ill. I have received a terrible shock. It will be my end, though. My days are numbered."

"Jekyll is ill, too. Have you seen him?" Utterson asked.

Lanyon's face changed and he held up a trembling hand. "I wish to see or hear no more of Dr. Jekyll," he said in a loud, unsteady voice. "I am quite done with him. He is dead to me, now."

"Tut-tut," said Mr. Utterson. After a considerable pause, the lawyer asked if he could do anything. "We are three old friends," Utterson pleaded. "One can never replace an old and dear friend."

"Nothing can be done," returned Lanyon. "Ask him yourself if you need further understanding."

"He will not see me," said the lawyer.

"I am not surprised," Lanyon said. "Some day, Utterson, after I am dead, you may come to understand some of this story. I cannot tell you. It is far too upsetting. In the meantime, if you would like to sit and talk about other subjects, then I would love you to stay. If you insist on discussing the case of Dr. Jekyll, then I must ask you to leave immediately."

Utterson stayed with his friend. They talked of old times and friends in common, everyone except Dr. Jekyll. After a few hours, the lawyer said good-bye and left his friend alone.

CHAPTER 12

A Letter from Dr. Lanyon

⌒

As soon as Utterson returned home, he wrote a letter to Dr. Jekyll. Utterson complained about being turned away repeatedly and expressed concern for Jekyll's health. He also asked the cause of Jekyll's unhappy break from Lanyon. The lawyer felt very frustrated. He was almost at his wits' end.

A reply arrived the next day. It was a long and sometimes confusing letter. Jekyll started his letter by saying that his break with Lanyon was permanent. "I do not blame him, of course," Jekyll wrote. "But I agree that he and I should never speak again. In truth, I intend to lead a life of seclusion from this day on. Please do not be hurt or upset if my door is closed even to you, Utterson. This is the way it must be. I have brought this punishment on myself. If I am the chief of sinners. I am also the chief of sufferers. Until this time, I had no idea that life could hold such agony. Utterson, if you wish to ease my pain in any way, then please respect my silence."

Utterson was amazed. Mr. Hyde and his evil influence were long gone. Not a week ago, Jekyll had been healthy, happy and heading toward a contented old age. They had returned to their routine of dinners together and evenings by the fire. Other friends had commented on Jekyll's fine spirits. Utterson had believed that the threat of Hyde was over and done with. Whatever could have happened in so short a time? Less than two weeks later, Dr. Lanyon died.

The church was filled with mourners, as Dr. Lanyon had many friends. Everyone was shocked by how quickly he had died. Only Utterson had suspected that the end was near. But of course, he said nothing to the other mourners. How would he ever explain the connection with Jekyll? Especially since Utterson felt that he, too, had been left in the dark.

The night after the funeral, Utterson sat alone in his den. Sitting by the light of a single candle, he pulled an envelope out of his pocket. Lanyon's lawyer had given it to him after the funeral. It read: "For the eyes of G.J. Utterson ALONE. If I, Dr. Lanyon, should outlive Mr. Utterson, this letter must be destroyed UNREAD." The lawyer bravely broke the seal on the envelope. Inside was another sealed envelope that read, "Not to be opened until the death or disappearance of Dr. Henry Jekyll." The wording shocked Utterson. This was the same as Jekyll's strange will concerning Mr. Hyde. It was Dr. Lanyon's hand-writing on the envelope. Why would Lanyon be concerned about Jekyll's disappearance? And why would Lanyon suspect that Jekyll might disap-pear one day? As both a trustworthy friend and lawyer, Utterson placed the sealed envelope in the farthest corner of his safe. He hoped the day would never come when he would have to open it. He feared the truth might be too hard to bear.

Utterson continued to call on Jekyll, but with less frequency. The lawyer had to admit to him-self that he was often relieved when Poole turned him away. He settled into a new routine and found comfort in it. Utterson knew that he would worry less if he kept busy.

On one of his visits to Jekyll's home, Utterson asked Poole if the doctor was feeling any better. The butler reported that his master was seen less and less, even within the household. Utterson noted that Poole looked worried.

"He spends most of his time in the room above the laboratory," Poole said. "In fact, Dr. Jekyll often sleeps there. I leave his meals outside the door and return later to retrieve the empty trays." Poole looked like he wanted to say more. He hesitated over a few words, then stopped. At last he said, "I'll tell the master that you were here."

Utterson thanked Poole and left. It was clear that Poole was worried about Jekyll's health and about how much time he spent alone. The lawyer was surprised to hear that even the doctor's servants rarely saw him. Utterson wondered if he had lost his good friend forever.

CHAPTER 13

Incident at the Window

෨

Despite the strange events of recent months, Utterson never missed his Sunday walk with Mr. Enfield. The lawyer took great pleasure in this ritual. There were times when he felt it was this connection to the world that kept him sane. His life had been so confusing and difficult, worrying over Jekyll's health. These walks reminded him of the time when his life felt normal. He missed his daily routines. Worrying so much about his friend was very tiring. Mr. Utterson hoped he would soon return to his simple life of quiet evenings at home and dinner parties with friends. He hoped that Jekyll would be better soon.

On one of these journeys, Utterson and Enfield once again happened upon the door where this story began. They both stopped to look at it. The door was still in need of a fresh coat of paint and the lock was damaged. It looked as though someone had tried to pry it open. Mr. Utterson thought about how much his life had changed since Enfield had first shown him this door. In a strange way, he felt responsible. Although he knew it made no sense, Utterson wondered if just hearing that story had led to everything that followed. Perhaps seeking out Hyde and looking for answers had caused more harm than good for Dr. Jekyll. Maybe Hyde had made things difficult for him. Jekyll might still be suffering the ill effects of Hyde's abuse and blackmail. Utterson was learning to accept that he might never know the truth.

"Well," said Mr. Enfield, "at least that story is at an end. We will hear no more of Mr. Hyde." The citizens of London still discussed the disappearance of Hyde. Nothing had been seen of him since the murder of Sir Danvers Crew. Many newspaper writers thought Hyde must have left England. There were rumors of sightings in Germany and France. One report had Hyde as far away as China, but there was no proof. Other people thought the criminal had escaped to Scotland. Then there were those people who thought he was still in London. They were certain that Hyde was waiting for right moment to come back and attack his next victim.

"I hope you are right," said Mr. Utterson. "Did I ever tell you that I met him once? I shared your feeling of disgust."

"I think it would be impossible not to," Enfield replied. "And, by the way, I apologize for not realizing sooner that this door was a back way into Dr. Jekyll's house. I knew he was your dear friend, of course, but I did not realize while I was telling you that upsetting story that the house belonged to Jekyll. I am deeply sorry if I offended you."

"Do not trouble yourself," Utterson said. "I must tell you, I am quite worried about Jekyll. He has not been well for some time. Would you mind if we stepped into the courtyard of his building?" Utterson asked. "I'd like to take a look at the windows."

"Of course," Enfield replied. "Perhaps we could encourage Jekyll to join us on our walk. The more the merrier, I say."

The courtyard was cool and a little damp. Although the afternoon sun was still high in the sky, twilight shadows fell inside the court. Dr. Jekyll's staff was careful about cleaning the courtyard and tending the flowers. Normally, it was filled with green plants and colorful flowers.

Utterson had spent many a happy afternoon sitting with Jekyll in the courtyard, talking for hours. On this day, though, it looked lonely from neglect. The leaves had turned brown from lack of water. There were no flowers to enjoy. Grass and weeds grew around the stones in the footpath. The birdbath was empty. Utterson knew this was not a good sign. Jekyll would never allow the yard to look so messy if he was healthy and happy.

The two men looked up at the windows above the laboratory. The middle one was slightly open. Sitting close behind it, slumped in a chair, was Dr. Jekyll.

"Hello! Jekyll!" Utterson called. "I trust you are feeling better?"

The doctor turned slowly toward the voice in the courtyard. He looked confused, as if he had no idea there was a world beyond his window. His eyes softened as he recognized his old friend.

"I am very low, Utterson," replied the doctor drearily. "Very low, indeed. It will not last long, thank God."

"You stay indoors too much," the lawyer said. "You should get some exercise. Why not join Mr. Enfield and me—have you met my cousin Mr. Enfield?—on our walk? Come now, get your hat and come outside."

"You are very kind," Jekyll called from the window. "I should like to but it's quite impossible. I dare not go outside." Dr. Jekyll tried to smile. "It is very good to see you, though," he said. "Very good, indeed. I would ask you and Mr. Enfield up, but the place is really not fit for visitors."

"We certainly don't want to trouble you, Dr. Jekyll," Enfield added. "My cousin has told me so much about you that I was looking forward to a visit.

"I'm very sorry to disappoint you," Jekyll replied. He sounded truly sorry. "I'm afraid we've missed the opportunity to enjoy each other's company."

"Then the best thing we can do is stay down there and talk with you," the lawyer said. He tried to sound happy and bright.

"I was just going to suggest the same thing," the doctor replied with a weak smile. But the words were hardly out of his mouth before his smile disappeared. An expression of complete horror quickly followed. Jekyll closed his eyes tightly. A grimace came across his face. He appeared to be in a great deal of pain. The two men watched in horror as his skin turned gray. Jekyll covered his face with his hands. He turned from the window and hunched over. They heard a low moan as he disappeared below the window frame.

The two men in the courtyard were shocked by what they saw. Utterson tried to call out to his friend, but no sound came. He was shocked and a bit frightened. A moment later the curtain was quickly drawn across the window. There was nothing they could do. The two men fled the courtyard without another word.

They continued in silence for several blocks. At last they looked at one another. They were both very pale. Utterson wanted to talk about what they had just seen. What had come over Jekyll as he sat by the window? What type of illness caused such a drastic change in his appearance? It had to be more than simple stress. The lawyer wondered if his friend had been poisoned. He knew that Jekyll's staff would never cause him harm. There was only one person who presented such a danger. Did this mean that Hyde was still nearby? Did he still have Jekyll under his control? The only thing Utterson knew for sure was that he and Mr. Enfield had just witnessed something awful. Mr. Utterson could only manage a few words. "God forgive us. God forgive us," he said.

Mr. Enfield only nodded his head very seriously. There were no words to describe what had happened. Enfield knew that no one would believe him if he tried. They walked on once more in silence.

CHAPTER 14

The Last Night

❧

Mr. Utterson was haunted by what he had seen in the window, yet felt powerless to do anything to help. He did his best to put the terrible image out of his mind. One night, however, as he was sitting by his fireside after dinner, he was surprised to receive a visit from Poole.

"My goodness, Poole, what brings you here?" Utterson cried. "Is Dr. Jekyll ill?"

"Mr. Utterson," the butler said. He was out of breath. Utterson wondered if the butler ran all the way over. "There is something terribly wrong."

The butler was very nervous. Mr. Utterson offered Poole a seat. "Please take your time," the lawyer said.

"You know the doctor's ways, sir," replied Poole. "You know how he shuts himself away. Well, he has locked himself in the office above the laboratory and I'm very worried. It's much worse this time. Mr. Utterson, I am afraid for my master's health. I think he may be in great danger."

"Now, my good man," Utterson said. "What exactly are you afraid of?"

"I've been afraid for about a week now," Poole said. "And I can bear it no more." The butler shook his head in frustration. He could not look the lawyer in the eyes. He sat with his hands on his knees to keep them from shaking. "I can bear it no more," he repeated.

"Poole," the lawyer said. "You must tell me

what has happened. Why are you so frightened for Dr. Jekyll?"

"I think there has been some foul play," said Poole, hoarsely.

"Foul play!" cried the lawyer. He jumped from his chair. Utterson's heart pounded in his chest. "What do you mean?"

"I can't say, sir," Poole said. "But will you come with me and see for yourself?"

Mr. Utterson answered by grabbing his coat and hat. He noticed the look of relief on Poole's face. The lawyer put his hand on the butler's shoulder. "We'll get to the bottom of this," Utterson said. The two men left the house.

It was a wild, unseasonably cold night. The men held their hats on against the wind. Dust and grit swirled through the air. Thin trees in the garden lashed themselves against the railing. Few people would brave such awful weather, so the streets were almost bare. Utterson thought the streets had never looked so lonely. He also felt a great sense of doom. He knew that this evening would bring something terrible. He feared the worst for Dr. Jekyll.

As they approached Jekyll's house, Poole took his hat off, despite the cold, to wipe his sweaty brow. Poole had been rushing the whole way, but now he paused. When he spoke, his voice was harsh and broken. "Well, sir," he said. "Here we are. I pray that all is well inside."

"Amen, Poole," the lawyer said.

Poole knocked on the front door with a code: three quick raps then two slow ones. The door opened only a few inches and a face peered out. "Is that you, Poole?" a woman's voice said.

"It's all right," Poole said. "Open the door."

Utterson and Poole entered the front room. It was brightly lit by a roaring fire. All the household servants were huddled together like a flock of sheep. At the sight of Mr. Utterson, one of the maids began to cry. The cook said, "It's Mr. Utterson!" She ran to him and threw her arms around his neck.

"Why are you all here?" the lawyer asked. He sounded irritated. The servants should not be gathered by the fire in the front room.

"They're all afraid," Poole said.

The room remained quiet. Only the sobs of the maid could be heard above the roaring fire.

"Jeremy," Poole said to a young man. "Hand me some candles. We should deal with this at once." Poole's voice was sharp. His nerves were clearly rattled.

"Mr. Utterson," Poole said. He took two lit candles from Jeremy and passed one to the lawyer. "Would you please follow me?" The butler then led the way through the house and into the courtyard.

CHAPTER 15

Poole's Story

⌣∽

"I must ask you to remain quiet, sir," Poole whispered as they walked. "I think it would be best if he didn't know you were here. Listening in would be best."

"I understand," Utterson said. It was hard for the lawyer to keep his hand from shaking. Candle wax dripped on his hand, but he made no noise.

He followed Poole to the top of the laboratory stairs. The butler indicated that he should stand to one side and listen. He took a deep breath, and knocked with a somewhat uncertain hand on the door.

"Sir," Poole called through the door. "Mr. Utterson is here to see you."

A voice answered from within. "Tell him I cannot see anyone," it said shakily.

"Thank you, sir," Poole answered. He seemed pleased with the voice's response. He started back down the stairs. Utterson followed behind him.

When they were once again in the courtyard, Poole turned back to the lawyer. "Now, tell me, sir," Poole said. "Was that my master's voice?"

"It seems much changed," answered Utterson, very pale.

"Well, I certainly think so," said the butler. "Could I work in this house for twenty years and not know my master's voice? No, sir. That voice is not my master's. Something has happened to him, or he has been taken away. It has been eight days now and I am at my wits' end."

"This is a very strange, Poole. It is rather a wild tale, my man," Utterson said. "Suppose you were right and Dr. Jekyll has been murdered or kidnapped. Why would the culprit stay in the room? Why wouldn't he escape?"

"You are a hard man to satisfy, Mr. Utterson, but I'll do my best to convince you," Poole said. "All this past week, he—or it—or whatever is locked in that office—has been crying night and day for special medicine. He writes orders for medicine on notes and leaves them on the stairs. This practice was continued all this week. Not just one or two notes, but dozens. I've traveled to pharmacies across the city, filling these orders and sending complaints. You see, every time I returned with the medicine I was told that it was not pure. I was told to return it and go to another pharmacy. I have no idea what the medicine is, but he is desperate for it."

"Do you have any of these notes?" Utterson asked.

Poole reached into a pocket and pulled out a crumpled piece of paper. The lawyer bent over his candle and carefully examined the writing. It read as follows: "I return this medicine purchased from your firm, as it is not pure and therefore useless to me. I purchased a large quantity some years ago. I am in desperate need to refill this order. I must ask you to carefully search your supplies to find a pure and proper sample. I can not stress enough the importance of this order." It was the last line of the note that disturbed Utterson the most. There was a sudden splash of ink as the author's emotions became too strong. "I beg you," the note read, "please find the medicine of old."

"This is a strange note," Utterson said. "Why is it open?" the lawyer asked rather sharply. It seems that Utterson would defend his friend Jekyll to the end. Even though he realized Poole was only trying to help, he was suspicious that Poole opened private notes.

"One of the pharmacists was so angry that he threw it back at me," Poole said.

"Do you recognize this as Dr. Jekyll's handwriting?" Utterson asked.

"It does look like it," the butler said rather sulkily. "But what does that matter when I've seen the man who wrote this?" Poole blurted out.

"Seen him?" Utterson said. "Where? When?"

"I stepped into the garden unexpectedly," Poole said. "He must have come out to look for a delivery of medicine. I saw him standing at the other end of the courtyard looking through crates. When he saw me, he let out a sharp cry and ran back up the stairs. I only saw him for a few minutes, but my blood ran cold at the sight of him. My hair practically stood on end. Sir, if that was my master, why did he scream out like a rat and run off?" Poole passed his hand over his face in great despair.

"These are all very strange stories," Utterson said. "But I think I'm beginning to see the light. Your master must be suffering some sort of breakdown. That would explain the change in his voice and avoiding his friends. He must believe that this mysterious medicine will cure him of this sickness. I do hope he is right in that matter and we can cure him."

"Sir," said the butler. "The creature in the office is not my master and that is that!" He looked around him then began to whisper. "My master is a tall, well-built man, while this person is much shorter and rather stooped. Do you think after all these years that I wouldn't notice where my master's head comes to in the doorway? Do you think I would not recognize his footsteps? No, sir, that thing was not—is not—Dr. Jekyll. I believe that my master has been murdered."

"Poole," the lawyer said, "are you quite certain that you believe this?" Utterson broke out into a sweat. It was an unbearable thought that his oldest and dearest friend was murdered. The butler nodded slowly. "We have only one option then. We must break down the door," Utterson said.

CHAPTER 16

The Other Side of the Door

୧୨

The butler agreed at once. "Ah, Mr. Utterson, that's talking!" he cried.

"How should we go about this?" Utterson asked. "We should arm ourselves. We never know what we might find inside the office."

The butler nodded. "There is a croquet mallet in the shed. May I suggest you take the fireplace poker, sir?"

Utterson thought for a moment that he might laugh. Tensions were high. It was hard to believe that he was in this situation. It felt like a passage from an adventure novel. Utterson could say without a doubt that he had never had an experience like this before. It was certainly not how he pictured his evening or the fate of his good friend Dr. Jekyll.

"Do you realize, Poole," he said, "that we are about to put ourselves in a situation of some danger?"

"You may say so, sir, indeed," returned the butler.

"We should be completely honest with one another right now," said Utterson. "Did you recognize the man you saw in the courtyard?"

"It's hard to say. It all happened so quickly. And he was doubled over when I saw him, so I can't say for certain," Poole said. "But if you're asking me whether or not it was Mr. Hyde, well, I'd have to say yes. It looked very much like him. I hate to think it, but it is true. Have you ever met Mr. Hyde?" Poole asked the lawyer.

"Yes," Utterson said. "I spoke with him once."

"Then you know the response Mr. Hyde brings out in people."

"I know it well," Utterson replied. "He literally sent shivers up my spine."

"I realize that it isn't proof," Poole whispered. "But when I saw that creature going through the crates, I had the same reaction. I went cold at the sight of him."

"Ah," Utterson sighed. "I fear that you may be right. If it was Mr. Hyde that you saw, then Henry Jekyll must surely be dead. Well, then, let's get to it!" The lawyer's heart sank. His hope of finding his friend safe and sound was quickly fading.

"Perhaps you should call the footman, Bradshaw, to stand guard," Utterson suggested. "We may need extra help."

Poole agreed and ran back into the house. Bradshaw arrived few moments later, pale and nervous. Although a large man, he was clearly frightened. He was sweating and nervously shifting from one foot to the other. He put his hands in his pockets so the other men wouldn't see them shaking.

"Pull yourself together, Bradshaw," Utterson said. "Poole and I are going to break down the office door. We don't know what we might find, or what might happen. There's a chance that the culprit will attempt an escape. Would you please stand guard by the back door?" Bradshaw nodded. "Fine. We'll give you a few minutes to get there." Utterson shook Bradshaw's hand before the footman walked off.

The two men remained in silence. Utterson looked into the night sky, admiring the stars and the heavens. *It really is quite remarkable*, he thought. *Life can provide so many twists and turns but the stars are always beautiful.* After a few minutes, Utterson took a deep breath.

"And now, Poole, we must be off on our task,"

Utterson said. The men walked across the court-yard, their candles flickering in the wind. As they walked up the stairwell they could hear pacing across the office floor.

"It's like this day and night," Poole said. "The only time the pacing stops is when new medicine arrives. Then, as soon as he realizes the batch isn't right, the pacing starts again."

"That is all you hear?" asked Utterson.

"Once I heard weeping, sir," Poole answered. "Weeping like a woman or a lost soul."

The two men gathered up their nerve outside the office door. Utterson grasped the fire poker in both hands and shouted. "Jekyll!" he said in a loud voice. "I demand to see you!" He paused a moment, but there was no reply. "I've given you fair warning. We must and shall see you," he resumed. "If not by fair means, then by foul. If not with your consent, then by brute force."

"Utterson," the voice said. "Please, have mercy!"

"Ah, that's not Jekyll's voice—it's Hyde's!" cried Utterson. "Down with the door, Poole!"

Poole used an axe to ram at the door hinges. The first strike let out a loud crash, shaking the door. The second and third strikes moved the door slightly. A horrible screeching sound was heard from within, like an animal under attack. Utterson and Poole looked at one another knowingly. They returned to the door with renewed force and determination. It was not until the fifth strike that the door came crashing down.

The two men peered into the room, afraid of what they might see. They were surprised to see a room full of fire and warmth. A kettle was boiling over the flames and dishes were laid out for tea. There was a blanket on a chair and a book open on a table as though someone had recently been sitting there. Some drawers in the cabinet

were open and papers were neatly piled on top the desk. It would have looked like the most common room in London except for the many chemicals and medicines along the shelves. And the body lying on the rug.

CHAPTER 17

Inside the Lab

∽

U tterson and Poole tiptoed closer to the body. They turned it over and found the face of Edward Hyde. He was dressed in clothes far too large for him. These clothes clearly belonged to Dr. Jekyll. Hyde was dead. His lifeless hand still clutched an empty vial. Utterson knew that it had once contained poison. This was clearly a case of suicide.

"We have come too late," Utterson said sternly. "Hyde is gone and we'll never have answers." The lawyer looked up at the butler.

"Now, it only remains for us to find the body of your master."

The two men started their search for Dr. Jekyll. They began with the office, then worked their way down the staircase and through the courtyard. There were many dark closets and a large cellar to search through. All were carefully examined. Most of these hiding spaces had not been visited in years. The dust along the walls and cobwebs told them that no one else had passed that way. They found no trace of Dr. Henry Jekyll, dead or alive.

"Perhaps we were wrong," Utterson said. "Maybe he escaped." He went to check the back door. It was locked. They found the key lying on the ground nearby. It was already stained with rust.

"This doesn't look like it's been used in a while," observed the lawyer.

"Used?" echoed the butler. "Do you not see,

sir? It is broken. It looks like someone has crushed it underfoot."

"Yes," continued Utterson. "I think you're right." The two men looked at each other with frightened stares. "This is beyond me," the lawyer said.

They walked back up the stairs in silence. Each man was deep in thought. They began to look through the contents in the office more closely. They both tried not to look at Hyde's body on the rug. Hyde must have been mixing chemicals together on one of the tables. They found several measuring glasses of salt and other chemicals. Utterson guessed that they had interrupted Hyde in the middle of an experiment.

"That is the same drug that I was always bringing him," said Poole. "Was Mr. Hyde performing the same experiments as Dr. Jekyll? Maybe the medicine was for Mr. Hyde all along."

The two men suddenly noticed that the kettle

was boiling and overflowing. They were so absorbed in their work that they noticed little else. Poole removed the kettle from the heat. Utterson approached the easy chair where the dishes for tea were laid out. He noticed a book on the table. It was a copy of a religious text that Jekyll often spoke of. There was writing along the margins. Utterson was shocked by what he read. It appeared to be in Jekyll's handwriting but the words seemed so unlike the doctor's.

A full-length mirror stood in the center of the room. It had a large wooden frame with its own stand. There was glass on both sides. Mr. Utterson spun the mirror by holding the top and turning it over. "Why would Jekyll want this mirror in his office?" he asked.

"I've no idea, sir," Poole said. "I've never seen it before."

They turned their attention to the desk. Among the neat array of papers, Utterson found an envelope addressed to him. It was in Dr. Jekyll's handwriting. The lawyer unsealed it and several other envelopes fell out. The first was a will. It contained the same strange terms as the one that sat in Utterson's safe. On this one, however, the lawyer was listed as the heir rather than Edward Hyde. Utterson looked at Poole, back at the paper, and then finally at the body on the floor.

"I am completely confused, Poole," Utterson said. "He's barely spoken with me in recent times. I'm shocked by this change."

Utterson picked up another paper. It was a note, written in the doctor's hand and dated that day. "Oh, Poole," he cried. "He was alive and here this very day. He must have fled! But why?"

"Why don't we read it, sir," Poole said.

Utterson took a deep breath and read the note aloud.

My dear Utterson,

When this note falls into your hands, I will have disappeared. Under what circumstances I cannot say. I am certain, however, that it will happen very soon and it will be some method of evil. Please go and read the letter that Lanyon sent you before his death. If you still wish to hear more, open the third envelope.

Your unworthy and unhappy friend,
Henry Jekyll

Poole handed Utterson the last envelope. It was very thick and sealed in several places.

The lawyer put the package in his pocket. "Please say nothing about this paper. If your master has fled or is dead, we may at least save his honor. It is now ten o'clock. I must go home and read these documents in quiet. I shall be back here before midnight, when we shall send for the police."

They left the office. Poole made certain the door from the house to the courtyard was locked so no one would wander back that way. "Please tell Bradshaw to remain at his post," Utterson said. "Dr. Jekyll may yet return and we don't want to miss him."

Utterson passed the servants still huddled by the great fire in the front room. They looked silently at him as he passed. He let himself out the front door and made his way home.

CHAPTER 18

A Letter from Dr. Jekyll

U tterson took the envelope out of his safe. He sat down heavily and began to read Dr. Lanyon's story.

"Four days ago, on January 9th, I received an evening delivery of a registered envelope. It was from my old friend, Dr. Henry Jekyll. I was very surprised by this, as we had never exchanged letters before. I had seen him the night before and did not expect contact so soon. I could not imagine what could be so important. My curiosity grew after reading the letter. It ran as follows:

Dear Lanyon,

You are one of my oldest friends. Although we have had our differences of late on scientific matters, I cannot remember any break in our affection. I am certain that you know I would never think twice about coming to your rescue. At a moment's notice I would be at your side. Lanyon, my life, my honor, and my reason are all at your mercy. If you fail me tonight, I am lost. You might suspect that I am about to ask you to do something shameful. Judge for yourself.

I ask that you put everything aside tonight— even if an emergency should arise—and bring this letter to my house. My butler has his orders. You will find him waiting with a locksmith. I need you to break into my office. Once the door is open, you should enter alone. Remove the far left drawer of the medicine cabinet. You will find it filled with some powders and vials. I am in such a state of panic and worry that I may misdirect you in some way.

Therefore, please take the entire drawer and all its contents with you. Take it back to your home. I will send someone to get it.

I am concerned about timing. If you leave for my home immediately after receiving this letter, then you should be home well before midnight. There is also the chance that you will be delayed in some way, so allowing you this extra time is best. I ask that you please be alone at midnight. No servants can be nearby. At midnight, then, I ask that you admit a man who will present himself in my name. Please give him the drawer that you have removed from my office. Your work will be done at this point. If you choose to have further explanation, all will be revealed in the next five minutes.

The mere thought of you refusing my request is too much to bear. My mind reels and I'm thrown into fits of panic. Think of me in this hour, in a strange

place, full of despair. I know that I am asking a lot
of you, but your willingness to help has done wonders
for my spirits.

Your friend,
Henry

"This letter convinced me that Dr. Jekyll was insane. However, I could take no chances. I knew that I must fulfill his wishes. I was not in a position to judge, since I did not know all of the details. And, in the end, the most important fact was that a friend was in great need. Therefore, I did as the letter asked and went directly to Jekyll's home. His butler was waiting for me with a locksmith. He had also received a letter by registered mail from Jekyll. We immediately went to work. It took some time, but the locksmith was at long last successful. The door to the office swung open. I pulled the second drawer from the left, as Jekyll requested.

"Once I had returned home I examined the drawer's contents. It was full of powders and vials just as he had said it would be. It was plain to me that these chemicals were of Jekyll's own making. I recognized none of them. The powder appeared to be some form of salt. The vials were full of a red liquid. It had a very strong odor, almost sickly sweet. I could make no guess at the name of the other chemicals. It was all very strange. The only thing to do now was wait. Eventually this man would come to pick up the drawer. I could not understand what these chemicals had to do with the safety and sanity of Jekyll. All of this convinced me more than ever that Jekyll was insane. I sent my servants to bed and waited in my lab for my midnight visitor."

CHAPTER 19

A Visit from a Stranger

"The bells had barely struck twelve o'clock when the stranger appeared at my door. I asked if Dr. Jekyll had sent him. He said yes, so I asked him inside. He looked behind him to make sure that no one saw him from the street. A policeman passed my house moments later. I noticed that this man watched at the window until the officer was gone.

"These details had me worried. I wondered what kind of man Jekyll had sent to my house. I thought it best to get this nasty task over with as soon as possible. I led him to my study, where I had left the drawer.

"I took a good look at this man. He was short and wore a heavy coat. It was his face that was the most striking, though. The only word I can use is horrible. It made my heart skip a beat at first glance. I was, however, curious. Perhaps it is because I am a doctor, but I could not look away. Why did his physical appearance affect me so strongly?

"These observations have taken some time to write down but they covered mere seconds in real life. We moved quickly from front hall to the study, as my visitor was very anxious to get the drawer.

"'Have you got it?' he cried. 'Have you got it?' He was so impatient that he started to shake me.

"I pushed him back a step or two. 'Come, sir,' I said. 'You forget that I have not yet had the pleasure of meeting you. Be seated, if you please.'

I sat down myself, doing my best to appear natural. I'm not certain why I delayed giving him the medicine. My curiosity got the best of me, I suppose. I wanted to see how he would react.

"'I beg your pardon, Dr. Lanyon,' he replied civilly enough. 'I realize that I am impatient, but I come at the request of your good friend Dr. Jekyll. I would not like to keep him waiting.' He paused and put his hand to his throat. I could see that, in spite of his collected manner, he was close to tears. 'I understand . . . that I am to retrieve . . . a drawer,' he sputtered.

"I took pity on my visitor. No, perhaps I was more interested in satisfying my own curiosity. It is hard to say at this point with all the information I now possess.

"'There it is, sir,' I said, pointing to the drawer where it lay on the floor.

"He sprang to it. Then he paused and laid his hand upon his heart. I could hear his teeth grinding with nerves. He plucked away the sheet. At the sight of the contents he uttered a sob of such great relief that I sat terrified. I was shocked when he spoke a moment later, asking for a measuring glass.

"I rose from my place with something of an effort and gave him what he asked.

"He thanked me with a smiling nod. He then proceeded to measure out a dose of the red liquid with the strange salt. As the ingredients came together, the mixture took on a bright color. It started to bubble and smoke. Then it turned a dark, rich purple and stopped churning. At last it slowly faded to a watery green color. My visitor watched each stage with a keen eye. He smiled and set the glass on the table. He then turned and looked at me sternly.

"'And now,' he said, 'will you be wise? Will you ask me to leave your house with this glass without further discussion? Or are you too

curious now? Think carefully before you decide. If you choose, I can leave and you will be neither richer nor wiser from the experience. Or I can stay and a new world of understanding will be opened up to you. A world you can hardly imagine at this point.'

"'Sir,' I said, attempting to sound cool and calm, although I was far from either. It was clear that he was challenging me, asking if I was brave enough to see this story through. 'I have gone too far in this strange business to turn back now. I must see the end."

"'Very well,' he said. 'Only keep your vows in mind. Remember that I gave you every opportunity to stay out of this. You have lived by such narrow views for so long now that you cannot understand the areas of science and wonder that surround you. Look!'

"He put the glass to his lips and drank it in one gulp. A cry followed. He reeled, staggered, clutched at the table and held on, staring with dazed eyes. And as I looked, a change came over him. He seemed to swell. His face began to alter. In the next moment, I had sprung to my feet and leapt back against the wall. My arm was raised to shield me from this sight. My mind was swimming in terror.

"'No, no!' I screamed, again and again. For there before my eyes—pale and shaken and half fainting—stood Henry Jekyll!

"What he told me in the next hour I cannot bring myself to repeat. I saw what I saw, I heard what I heard, and my soul is sickened by it. Yet now that he is not before me, I wonder if it was true. It seems far too strange. I cannot answer. My life is shaken to its roots. Sleep has left me. The deadliest terror sits by me at all hours of the night and day. Every noise makes me jump. I am frightened of shadows and darkness. I feel that my days are numbered, that I must die. Jekyll claimed regret and sorrow—he even shed tears—but I doubt whether that would be enough. I will say but one thing, Utterson, and that will be more than enough. The creature who crept into my house that night was, by Jekyll's own confession, known by the name of Hyde and hunted in every corner of the land as the murderer of Sir Danvers Carew."

CHAPTER 20

A Transformation

꿍

Utterson put down Lanyon's letter and turned to the last envelope. He held it in his hands a few moments before opening it. He knew this letter would be his final contact with Henry Jekyll. He was both curious and worried by what his friend would have to say. Utterson slowly opened the envelope, unfolded the thick stack of papers, and began to read.

"I was born to a large fortune. I had a love of industry and study, and enjoyed the company of friends. All indications were that my life would be blessed with good fortune and promise. No one doubted that I was headed toward a great career. Indeed, my only fault was my rather free-spirited nature. It was always a great difficulty for me to hide my joy of life and display a more noble outlook. According to my family, it was considered impolite to appear too lively, too enthusiastic. I learned to hide my pleasures. I was one person when with my family and someone else when on my own. It wasn't until I was in my mid-twenties that I took stock of my surroundings and realized that I was leading a double life. Some men might have bragged about their exploits, but I saw them as shameful secrets. I took great pains to hide them from the world. Over time I had succeeded in dividing the two sides of my nature, the good and the evil. I was in no sense a liar, as both sides of me were true. I was entirely myself when engaging in some shameful activity, just as I was entirely myself while living a good and clean life. My scientific studies centered on this dual nature of man, that we can be both good and bad. I assumed that there was a logical and chemical reason for this division. It must be a part of our physical makeup. Why is one person blond and the other brunette? Why are some people tall and others short? There must be a similar reason to explain the good and bad parts of mankind. I was my own lab experiment. Every day I felt I was drawing closer to understanding this division. It was my strong belief that man is not one, but two. Two persons in one. I am certain that other scientists will follow and discover that we are in fact even more than two. For now, though, I must stick with what I know to be true. During my studies and experiments, I became convinced that this dual nature could be separated. I told myself that if each side of a person could be divided into separate identities, life would be easier. The evil could go in one direction and the good in the other. We would easily recognize one from the other. There would be no more uncertainty or confusion. That these two opposing forces trapped within the same body had already caused too much pain. My next question was, 'How could I separate them?'

"I will not go into the exact scientific details of my discovery for two reasons. First, I believe that it is too dangerous to pass on such information. We are all naturally curious and I would not want anyone else to be harmed. Second, as you will soon learn from my confession, my discoveries were incomplete. Needless to say, after much experimenting and trial and error, I discovered what I thought to be the perfect combination.

"I waited some time before I put this theory into practice. I knew well that I risked death. Any drug that shakes the very idea of who we are must be dangerous. But my curiosity was too great. Any concerns I had were overcome by my intense desire to learn something new. I purchased a large quantity of a particular salt from a wholesale company. I knew this salt was the last piece to the puzzle. Late one night, I put all the elements together in a measuring glass. I watched as it bubbled, smoked, and boiled. It changed colors several times before turning a pale watery green. Taking a deep breath for courage, I swallowed the potion quickly.

"The pain and sickness surprised me. I found myself rolling on the floor in agony. I felt certain that I had done myself serious harm. Then, quite suddenly, the pain stopped. I felt perfectly fine. I stood up and realized that I felt lighter, healthier, younger than I had in years. I had a strange feeling of restlessness. New, strange, and, dare I say, wicked images flashed through my mind. I believe wicked is the right word to use here. I felt positively wicked and free from any duty. I stretched out my arms and noticed for the first time that I was shorter. Somehow, I had shrunk during my transformation. My clothes were all too big for me now. I had become Mr. Edward Hyde."

CHAPTER 21

A New Perspective

ᥱᥱ

"I had no mirror in the lab. I eventually installed one in my office so I could watch the transformation. The first night, however, I had to sneak inside my own house. As I skulked across the courtyard, I noticed that the sky was full of stars. It occurred to me that in all of their millions of years in existence, they had never looked down on such a being like me before. I also knew that if my servants found me wandering through the corridors, they would summon the police. Looking into a hall mirror, I saw a dried-up and ugly face. I wondered if the evil in a man's soul could affect a face so strongly. My first guess was yes. There could be no other explanation for Hyde's awful appearance. It would seem that my "evil side" was not as developed as my good side. Of course, this only makes sense, since I had never allowed it time to grow or exercise. I had spent most of my life hiding it away, keeping it locked up and quiet. I wasn't disgusted, though. I recognized the reflection in the mirror as me. It was still me that I was looking at. This was unlike anyone else's reaction. Every single person—even you, my good friend Utterson—jumped back when he saw Edward Hyde. I think this is because people are used to looking at a person with both good and evil inside him, the dual nature I spoke of earlier. Edward Hyde, however, was like no other. He was pure evil.

"It was only then that the horrible thought occurred to me. What if I could not revert to my other self? I raced back to my laboratory. Quickly, I prepared the mixture again and drank it down. Again I was struck by terrible pains and spasms.

When I recovered, I was relieved to see that I had returned to the body of Dr. Henry Jekyll.

"Please believe that my plan were noble. I approached this experiment with purely scientific motives. But once I had reached a crossroads, I could not turn back. Something was unleashed in me. Perhaps it was simply curiosity. I'm afraid that I don't really know myself. Once I had discovered Mr. Hyde, he demanded to be let out more and more. He began to take root in the rest of my life.

"This change didn't happen overnight. I was

still involved in my studies. I still saw friends and associates. Over time, though, I could feel Mr. Hyde growing in strength. He was developing rapidly. I was intrigued at first, but Mr. Hyde's presence was to become unwelcome. I was obsessed by this power. Knowing that with a quick drink of potion I could switch between the bodies of an evil villain and a gentleman doctor was too much for one man. It became a form of torture. It became more and more difficult for me to meet with others. I let friendships slip away. Only my servants kept me company. Hyde, on the other hand, was not hidden away. He lived a life among thieves and monsters. That was the perfect company for Mr. Hyde.

"I—or perhaps I should say Hyde—rented that room in Soho. It was a place for him to stay in comfort and do whatever business he saw fit. In the meantime, I told all of my servants to admit Hyde into the house. I next drew up the will that bothered you so much. I worried that something might happen to my Jekyllside. I didn't want Hyde to be without money. Once I thought all sides had been taken care of, I actually began to enjoy the freedom of Mr. Hyde.

"Hyde could do anything he liked and no one would blame Jekyll. Hyde could commit unspeakable, awful acts, but it would never be the fault of Dr. Jekyll. There were times when I—as Jekyll—tried to repair the damage done by Mr. Hyde, so I was not without feelings. Your cousin Enfield may have told you a story about Hyde causing injury to a young girl. I paid her family a large sum of money. I know that the check could not undo the harm, but it was all I felt I could do. For the most part, though, I turned a blind eye."

CHAPTER 22

The Uncontrollable Mr. Hyde

"Two months before the murder of Sir Danvers, I returned from one of Hyde's adventures. I switched back to Jekyll and went to bed. I woke up with a very odd feeling. I recognized the room around me as my own, but something was wrong. I felt as though I was not in the right place. I lay on my bed wondering about this situation. I was convinced that there must be some logical and scientific answer to my discomfort. I was deep in thought when I noticed my hand. It was not the hand of Dr. Henry Jekyll. It was thin with sharp, large knuckles. It was the hand of Mr. Edward Hyde.

"I must have stared at that hand for nearly a minute. I was so caught up in the wonder of it all. When it finally all came together for me, I jumped out of bed and ran to the mirror. I could not believe my eyes. Yes, I had gone to bed as Henry Jekyll and woken up as Edward Hyde. How could this have happened? The next, perhaps more immediately important question, was how could this be remedied? It was mid-morning. All the servants were up and the medicine was in the laboratory. There was no way I could walk across the courtyard to get it. I would be able to cover my face, but that would not disguise me enough. Thankfully, I took a breath and realized that my servants were already used to Hyde's coming and going. I dressed quickly and left the room. I passed Bradshaw, the footman, who was taken aback by the presence of Hyde so early in the day. My loose-fitting clothes must also have caught his eye. Mr. Hyde disappeared across the courtyard. Ten minutes later, Dr. Jekyll was sitting down to breakfast, pretending to be interested in food.

"I knew that I would not be able to continue with my double life. I was losing control over it. Hyde was too developed now. I suspected that he had actually grown in strength. I had changed from Jekyll to Hyde without taking the medicine. My mind—or my body, I don't know which—switched on its own. The medicine was already losing its power. I had to drink three times as much medicine to switch back and forth. When I started this experiment, it was difficult to leave the Dr. Jekyll side behind. Now it was quite the opposite. The events of that morning confirmed that it was now more difficult to lose Mr. Hyde. It was clear that I was losing hold on my original and better self. My evil, criminal side was becoming too strong.

"I knew that I must choose between the two. Jekyll was worried and curious about Hyde's actions and well-being. Hyde was completely indifferent to Jekyll. Losing Hyde meant losing certain evils that I had grown to enjoy. But leaving Jekyll behind meant that I would be friendless and hated by all. I knew I could not live with that outcome.

"So I left Hyde behind. I still kept the apartment in Soho and Hyde's clothes hung in the closet of my laboratory, but I did not use the medicine. For two months I led a quiet and careful life. And I was happy with this life for a while. My conscience was clear. But the desires and instincts were not gone, only resting. I once again found myself mixing, then drinking, the potion.

"My devil had been long caged. Hyde arrived

with a roar and a fury that I had not expected. Even while I was drinking the potion I knew this time would be different. I knew that Hyde wanted to make up for lost time. And it was in this state that Hyde came upon Sir Danvers in the laneway. My memory of the event is weak. Hyde was in a blind rage. It all happened so quickly.

"I am to blame for all of this, because it was Hyde who performed the awful deed, but please believe this is not something Jekyll could have even considered. I knew that my life was over at that moment, too. Hyde, or I, fled from the scene. I ran to the apartment in Soho. I burned all my papers to destroy any evidence. Then I started to roam the streets of London. Hyde contemplated other murders he would like to perform. Now that he had the taste of one, I feared he would not stop.

"As soon as I became Jekyll again, I fell to my knees and begged God for mercy. I knew that there could be no more Hyde. Making this final decision felt like freedom. I hadn't even realized how much it felt like a prison. To make sure that I wouldn't be tempted and Hyde would not be able to walk through the back door, I broke the lock. Then I crushed the gate key underfoot.

"I learned the next day that my own maid was a witness to the murder. I was horrified to hear Hyde named as the killer. I hadn't even realized it was Sir Danvers that I met in the alley. Hyde's fury was so strong that my Jekyll side was completely overwhelmed. My evil side—Mr. Hyde—had complete control of my body and mind.

"I resolved to live the life of a reformed man. I began charity work. I attended regular church services and renewed old friendships. I returned from my solitude with full force. I was a man reborn. It felt like a miracle to be given this second chance. I had no idea that it would not last.

"One day in early spring, I was enjoying some

time on a park bench. I sat alone listening to the birds in the trees and watching the children play. I was suddenly struck by a wave of sickness and the most awful shuddering. This passed away and left me faint. I felt my temperature rising. I closed my eyes, hoping this feeling would also pass. I felt strange, though. I had a sudden race of energy. I could feel myself swiftly becoming angry. I opened my eyes again. My clothes looked suddenly too big. My hands were thin and pale. I was once again Edward Hyde.

"I knew that I could not sit out in the open like that. Hyde was a wanted man. I also knew that I had to get to my medicine. I couldn't walk up to the front door. Poole would call the police as soon as he saw me. I could not enter through the back door, since I had destroyed the lock and key. I knew that I was going to need help. That is when Dr. Lanyon came to mind. I wrote a letter to Lanyon asking him to retrieve my medicine. I knew that he would. You must know the events of that evening by now. Lanyon said that he would write you, so I won't repeat the story here. You must understand, though, that I was shocked by Lanyon's reaction. I expected him to be angry, but not horrified. The fact that this shock killed him is something I will always have to live with.

"A new fear was starting to take hold. It was no longer simply the police that I feared. I was terrified that I might be forced to live as Hyde. I hoped that I had seen the end of him. But the next day while walking across the courtyard I was struck by the familiar pangs. I took a double dose of the medicine and returned to the body of Dr. Jekyll. Then six hours later, while I was reading by the fire, the fear came again. I drank still more medicine. If I fell asleep—even for a nap—I always woke up as Mr. Hyde. I was horrified. This terror consumed me. As Jekyll grew weaker, Hyde became stronger. It took all my strength as

Jekyll to force Hyde to take the medicine. I fear this won't be possible for much longer. My supply of salt that I used in the potion had never been refilled. During this time, I had been using the same supply. I started to search for more. I had assumed that my original batch was a pure form of the salt. I therefore began to demand from the pharmacists the purest batch that they had. It was never right, though. I sent every batch back. I have since come to realize that my first batch was probably not the pure version. It must have been mixed with an unknown substance. It was this mystery substance, or its combination with the salt, that brought on the desired effect.

"About a week has passed since I started this letter. I am working under the influence of the last of the potion. This will most likely be the last time Henry Jekyll is allowed to speak or be heard. I must finish this letter now. I am concerned Hyde will take over before I have a chance to seal it. He will surely rip it to pieces if he sees it. This is my true hour of death. As I lay down my pen and go on to seal up my confession, I bring the life of an unhappy Henry Jekyll to an end.

May the good Lord take mercy on me,

Dr. Henry Jekyll"

What Do *You* Think?
Questions for Discussion

ᴄ᷍ꝋ

Have you ever been around a toddler who keeps asking the question "Why?" Does your teacher call on you in class with questions from your homework? Do your parents ask you questions about your day at the dinner table? We are always surrounded by questions that need a specific response. But is it possible to have a question with no right answer?

The following questions are about the book you just read. But this is not a quiz! They are designed to help you look at the people, places, and events in the story from different angles. These questions do not have specific answers. Instead, they might make you think of the story in a completely new way.

Think carefully about each question and enjoy discovering more about this classic story.

1. When Mr. Enfield tells Utterson his story, he is very mysterious about the owner of the house. Why do you suppose this is? Have you ever kept a secret from someone?

2. Dr. Jekyll's will states that, upon his death or disappearance, everything he owns should go to Mr. Hyde. Do you think this was a strange request? What's the strangest thing anyone has ever asked of you?

3. After killing Danvers Carew, Hyde returns home and destroys all of his papers. Why do you think he does this? Have you ever tried to hide or destroy evidence of something you shouldn't have done?

4. In spite of his strange behavior, Utterson continues to defend Jekyll. Why do you think he does this? Do you have a friend whom you would defend regardless of the situation?

5. Did you suspect that Jekyll and Hyde were actually the same person? Have you ever pretended to have a secret identity?

6. Jekyll claims that, after a time, changing into Hyde was beyond his control. Has anything ever happened to you that you couldn't control? How did you deal with it?

7. Throughout the book, Utterson is given a number of letters and told not to read them until specific events occur. How does he react to this? Would you have been able to stop yourself from reading the letters?

8. Hyde says to Lanyon, "If you choose, I can leave...or I can stay and a new world of understanding will be opened up for you." Why do you

suppose Lanyon chose as he did? What choice would you have made?

9. Utterson initially thinks that Jekyll forged the note from Hyde. Why do you think he came to that conclusion? Have you ever made a wrong assumption?

10. Jekyll says that we are all two people. What do you think he means? Do you agree?

Afterword

⌐∞

First impressions are important.

Whether we are meeting new people, going to new places, or picking up a book unknown to us, first impressions count for a lot. They can lead to warm, lasting memories or can make us shy away from any future encounters.

Can you recall your own first impressions and earliest memories of reading the classics?

Do you remember wading through pages and pages of text to prepare for an exam? Or were you the child who hid under the blanket to read with a flashlight, joining forces with Robin Hood to save Maid Marian? Do you remember only how long it took you to read a lengthy novel such as *Little Women*? Or did you become best friends with the March sisters?

Even for a gifted young reader, getting through long chapters with dense language can easily become overwhelming and can obscure the richness of the story and its characters. Reading an abridged, newly crafted version of a classic novel can be the gentle introduction a child needs to explore the characters and story line without the frustration of difficult vocabulary and complex themes.

Reading an abridged version of a classic novel gives the young reader a sense of independence and the satisfaction of finishing a "grown-up" book. And when a child is engaged with and inspired by a classic story, the tone is set for further exploration of the story's themes, characters, history, and details. As a child's reading skills advance, the desire to tackle the original, unabridged version of the story will naturally emerge.

If made accessible to young readers, these stories can become invaluable tools for understanding themselves in the context of their families and social environments. This is why the *Classic Starts* series includes questions that stimulate discussion regarding the impact and social relevance of the characters and stories today. These questions can foster lively conversations between children and their parents or teachers. When we look at the issues, values, and standards of past times in terms of how we live now, we can appreciate literature's classic tales in a very personal and engaging way.

Share your love of reading the classics with a young child, and introduce an imaginary world real enough to last a lifetime.

Dr. Arthur Pober, Ed.D.

Dr. Arthur Pober has spent more than twenty years in the fields of early-childhood and gifted education. He is the former principal of one of the world's oldest laboratory schools for gifted youngsters, Hunter College Elementary School, and former Director of Magnet Schools for the Gifted and Talented for more than 25,000 youngsters in New York City.

Dr. Pober is a recognized authority in the areas of media and child protection and is currently the U.S. representative to the European Institute for the Media and European Advertising Standards Alliance.

Explore these wonderful stories in our
Classic Starts library.